First published in this edition 1972 by William Collins
Sons and Co. Ltd., Glasgow and London

Printed in England
ISBN 0 00 138001 X

Treasure Trove Series

ANIMAL STORIES

Illustrated by Eric Kincaid

CONTENTS

COLLINS · GLASGOW AND LONDON

Mule Jingle

Jade Mule looked sadly at the pretty, woolly clouds, and sighed: "Why am I so plain and stubborn? I wish I were beautiful and nimble."

"Don't be sad, Jade," soothed Woolpack Cloud.

Jade neighed: "Tim and Julie, the Gamekeeper's children, think I'm stubborn. Tim said: 'Don't be as stubborn as a mule'."

Woolpack Cloud called: "He didn't mean it. You're as good as Betsy Donkey-on-the-Sand. I'm floating to the seaside to see her. Good-bye."

Julie and Tim Gamekeeper had also seen Betsy Donkey-on-the-Sand. They had only just come back from their August holiday, looking very suntanned. Jade had seen a photograph of Betsy with Julie on her saddle. They were trotting happily on the seashore. Betsy had some bells jingling around her neck.

As Julie filled Jade's cart, she said: "You ought to have bells jingling around your neck instead of this halter." Groaning, Jade slowly pulled his heavy cartload of wood to the Gamekeeper's house. "Never mind! At least you do bring us plenty of firewood, even though it takes you a long time," laughed Julie.

Now, all the birds in the wood noticed how miserable Jade Mule looked. They decided to have a picnic by a little stream on the edge of the wood. Jade was going to be invited, too.

After they had made preparations, the birds twittered until they had made a lovely necklace of Forget-Me-Nots.

Carrying it carefully, they flew to Jade, who was drooping his head unhappily.

With a start he jerked his head up as the birds arranged the Forget-Me-Not necklace on his neck. "Come to our picnic, Jade!" chirped the birds excitedly.

"Me? Where?" stammered Jade.

"Follow us," they chirped.

He trotted after the birds, in and out of the trees and through the woods, the dry dust settling on his hooves like sand. When they reached the stream they unpacked the picnic hamper, which Darty Kingfisher had prepared—bread, fruit cake, berries, grubs, insects, and grass and vegetables for Jade.

After eating and drinking, Nightingale smoothed his grey waistcoat and started singing a most beautiful song. Then two black and white Wagtails danced together, wagging their long tails while Willow Wren warbled sweet music. A little Dabchick, with rusty red throat and breast, gave a wonderful diving display in the slowly moving water. Green Woodpecker showed how quickly he could hammer as he clung to a tree. The visiting Skylark, who lived in a field, soared into the sky like an aeroplane, trilling sweetly.

Nod, nod, went Jade's head in time to the music. He *was* enjoying himself.

"Now it's your turn, Jade," the birds chirped.

"Me? But what can I do?" said Jade sadly.

"We'll show you," twittered the birds.

Jade snorted in surprise, as they all perched on his back. "Gee-up!" they all chirped happily.

Jade began to smile. Hmm! He could *pretend* to be a seaside donkey jingling on the sands. So, flicking his tail, he neighed: "One-two-three—off!"

The birds sang merrily as they clung to him. Trotting joyfully Jade forgot he was just a plain, stubborn mule.

When the tired but happy woodlanders went home Jade Mule dreamed happily of the day's events. After that, each time he pulled his cart he pretended to be a seaside donkey jingling along. And Jade never heard the word 'stubborn' again.

The Kitten Who Hated His Nose

Pepper was a fat, fluffy kitten, who lived in the country with a little boy named Andrew, and Andrew's Father and Mother. Pepper had a coat of yellow fur which shone like silk, and bright twinkling eyes the colour of barley sugar. He was much prettier than any of his friends who lived round about, excepting Carrots, who was a yellow kitten, too.

Pepper and Carrots looked so much alike that they might have been brothers, but Carrots lived on the farm beyond the hedge at the top of Andrew's garden. He was Pepper's best friend, and they often played together, or sat quietly, talking of important things, such as cream, and mice, and big, shaggy dogs.

One lovely spring morning, Pepper was sitting on a big upturned flowerpot washing his face, while Carrots, perched with great dignity on top of the dustbin, was telling him how much milk he had drunk for breakfast.

"Three saucersful, Pepper!" he said, licking his lips to show how much he had enjoyed it.

"You are lucky!" miaowed Pepper, carefully washing behind his right ear. "I only had one this morning."

"Well," said Carrots, "it must have been very good milk, for it's made your fur shine like silk. You know, Pepper, you really are a very pretty kitten!"

Pepper was beginning to purr with pleasure, when Smudge, the big black cat from next door, strolled up the garden path with Tabitha, the tabby cat who lived nearby. Smudge had a rather proud smile on his face.

"You *would* be a pretty kitten, Pepper," he remarked, "if it were not for your nose. You can't see it for yourself, of course, so you probably don't even know it's pink, but it is, isn't it, Tabitha?" Tabitha miaowed in agreement.

"All the best cats," went on Smudge, "have noses to match their fur. Look at mine. It's black, like my coat!"

"And look at mine," added Tabitha. "It's grey, like my stripes!"

Pepper looked, and sure enough their noses *did* match their fur. He shut one eye and tried to see his nose, but he could not. He shut the other eye, but that was no use either. He was very worried indeed. In fact, he was so worried that he quite forgot to wash behind his left ear.

"Don't worry about them, Pepper," said Carrots kindly. "Almost all yellow cats have pink noses. Haven't you noticed mine?"

"No," answered Pepper, looking eagerly at Carrot's nose. "Why, so it is!" he said, and he was so pleased that his friend had a pink nose, too, that he turned round and round on the flowerpot, chasing the tip of his fluffy tail.

"It isn't a bright pink nose like Pepper's though," said Smudge. "It's more like a raspberry in the middle of your face than a proper nose!"

"That's right," giggled Tabitha, "more like a raspberry!"

Pepper stopped chasing his tail at once, and began to worry again.

"It's very rude to make personal remarks like that," Carrots said crossly.

Tabitha stretched herself, and yawned without bothering to put her paw in front of her mouth. (They really were very ill-mannered cats!) "It's a great pity!" she said, as she walked away.

"Yes, a great pity!" echoed Smudge. "It quite spoils your beauty." And he walked away, too.

"Take no notice of them, Pepper," said Carrots, "and do cheer up! Your nose is very nice as it is!" He jumped off the dustbin and ran up the garden chasing a butterfly, but it flew up high and disappeared over the garden wall.

Now Pepper was all alone, sitting on the flowerpot wondering what he could do about his nose, because it looked like a raspberry, it did not match his fur, and he HATED it.

Could he dip it in the honey jar or the syrup tin in the larder? They were both yellow and would match his fur. Somehow or other it did not seem a very good idea, because honey and syrup were both terribly sticky, and Pepper could not bear to feel sticky. No, he must think of something else.

He thought hard for a very long time. He sat so still that a blackbird came hopping down the garden looking for worms, and did not even notice the kitten at all—and Pepper was much too unhappy to bother about chasing birds just then. He was still sitting on the flowerpot when a big bumble bee buzzed round his head. The kitten did not like the buzzy noise at all, so he jumped down and scampered up the garden, through the hedge, across the orchard and under Farmer Russett's five-barred gate into the farmyard, where Carrots lived. He decided that he would ask some of the animals what he could do about his pink nose; they would be sure to help him.

Pepper came first to the pig-sty, where Mr and Mrs Pig lived with their ten piglets. They were all busy having dinner, and made a slushy noise as they ate their food. The greedy little pigs squealed and pushed each other about as they tried to get a bigger share of the food, while Mr and Mrs Pig told them, in their strange, grunty language, to behave as nice piglets should.

Pepper waited politely until they had eaten every scrap and licked the trough quite clean. Then he said, in his small, squeaky voice: "Please, Mrs Pig, will you tell me how I can make my nose yellow, like my fur?"

Mrs Pig trotted up to the gate of the sty and looked closely at Pepper with her beady, black eyes.

"Why do you want a yellow nose?" she grunted. "It looks very nice as it is."

Then Mr Pig, with his ten piglets, came to look at Pepper's nose, too.

"Yes," grunted Mr Pig, "very nice as it is," and the fat piglets squealed to show that they agreed, too.

"But it's *pink*," complained Pepper, "and my friends

say it spoils my beauty, because it doesn't match my yellow fur."

Mr Pig snorted crossly, and went back to make sure that the trough was really empty, while the piglets pushed their snouts under the bar of the gate hoping to find something more to eat. But Mrs Pig was very angry.

"Pink noses *are* beautiful," she snorted. "We've all got pink noses in our family, and we wouldn't change them for *anything*!" Mrs Pig grunted so loudly that Pepper was frightened, and he ran off as fast as his little legs could carry him, across the farmyard to where the rabbits lived in their big wooden hutch.

Three fat, furry rabbits were enjoying some juicy lettuces for dinner. They had their backs to Pepper and he could see that each one had a fluffy, white tail, round as a little snowball. Pepper sat down and curled his own long tail right round his feet, and thought how funny it must be to have only a little fluffy ball for a tail.

"Please," he said after a while, "will you be kind enough to tell me how I can make my nose yellow, like my fur?"

The rabbits turned round in surprise, and came hopping to the wire netting at the front of their hutch to take a good look at Pepper.

"Why do you want a yellow nose?" asked one rabbit. "It looks very nice as it is."

"Yes," agreed the other two rabbits together, "it looks very nice as it is!"

Pepper stamped his little feet crossly. "But it's pink instead of yellow, and I HATE it," he miaowed. "It spoils my pretty face."

The rabbits put their furry heads right up against the

wire netting. "We have pink noses, too, but our fur is grey, and we think they're very pretty," they told him.

Pepper looked, and saw three pink, twitching noses, and what is more those three rabbits were laughing at him. He ran away, crosser than ever, right to the other end of the farm and into the meadow. There were some big, brown cows, chewing contentedly in the warm sunshine, and several horses nibbling at the soft, green grass.

Pepper went up to a big, brown cow standing in the shade of the hedge and said hullo rather nervously.

"MOO!" replied the friendly cow, so loudly that Pepper was terrified and scampered off across the meadow to where a huge black horse was nibbling grass.

"Hullo," miaowed the kitten politely. The black horse stopped nibbling, and looked at Pepper; then he lifted his great head in the air, opened his mouth and neighed.

"There," Pepper told himself, "*he's* laughing at my pink nose, too! Oh dear! Whatever *can* I do?" He crept away and walked slowly back towards the farmyard.

Two brown calves standing by the hedge looked at Pepper as he came towards them. "Hullo," he miaowed sadly.

"Moo!" replied the calves gently.

"I wonder," began the kitten, "if you can tell me how I can make my nose yellow, like my fur?" The calves looked very surprised.

"Why," said one, "whatever do you want to change the colour of your nose for? It looks very nice as it is."

"Yes," agreed the other, "it looks very nice as it is."

"But it's *pink*, and my friends tell me it spoils my beauty," explained Pepper. "Didn't you hear that big, black horse laughing at it just now?"

"He wasn't laughing at you," said one calf kindly. "He's always laughing. He laughs because he's happy!"

"It's all very well for him to be happy," grumbled Pepper. "His nose is black as coal, like his coat; not pink, like mine!"

"Moo!" said the calves both together. "We've got pink noses which don't match our coats, and we don't mind at all; we're very happy," and they kicked their little heels up into the air and raced off round the meadow, to show Pepper just how happy they were.

The kitten watched them go. Then he crept under the hedge and back into the farmyard, just as Mrs Russett came out of the house carrying a plate of dinner and a bone for Rufus, the farm dog. Rufus wagged his tail and barked with pleasure, because he was very hungry.

Pepper suddenly felt very hungry, too. It must be his

dinner time by now, so he'd better hurry home or he would be late. He waited until Mrs Russett turned to go into the house, before he started back across the yard. Then he ran, quick as a flash over to the pig-sty and round the corner. But, oh dear me! Who should he meet but Farmer Russett himself, coming back for his mid-day meal. The farmer bent down and picked him up.

"Ah-ha," laughed the kindly farmer, stroking the kitten gently, "where do you think you're off to, Carrots? Don't you want any dinner today?"

Pepper miaowed and struggled, trying to tell Farmer Russett that he was not Carrots at all, and that he lived with a little boy named Andrew, but the farmer did not seem to understand, for he carried him into the farmhouse.

A spaniel puppy and a young collie dog ran up excitedly as he went indoors, and when they saw the strange kitten he was carrying in his arms, they barked loudly and jumped up, trying to reach it.

Poor Pepper! He had never felt so frightened in all his life. He dug his little claws in the farmer's jacket and held on as tightly as he could.

"Now then! Now then! What's all the fuss about?" laughed Farmer Russett. "You don't usually take any notice of Carrots!" The two dogs kept barking and jumping up at the terrified little kitten. "Oh, well," said the farmer, "if you're going to make a noise like that, I shall have to shut Carrots in the kitchen, or he'll get no peace!"

He carried Pepper through the hall and into the kitchen, shutting the dogs outside. Then he put a dish of food on the floor.

"There you are, little Carrots," he said, putting the kitten down beside the dish. "Now, eat your dinner while I go and have mine." And he went to have his meal in the dining-room with Mrs Russett, leaving Pepper alone in the kitchen.

Although the dish was full of Pepper's favourite dinner—chopped liver and gravy—the poor little kitten was much too frightened to feel hungry now.

If *only* he hadn't come to the farm! If *only* he had not minded what those silly cats said about his pink nose! Lots of animals at the farm had pink noses which did not match their coats, and they did not mind at all—they were quite happy. If *only* he could get out of this house and away from those fierce dogs, he would be happy, too. He would never, *never,* come near the farm again.

Pepper could hear the dogs sniffing under the door, and he could hear Farmer Russett and his wife talking in the next room while they ate their dinner.

"Whatever is the matter with those dogs today?" he heard Mrs Russett ask the farmer.

"I've no idea," he replied. "They barked and jumped up when I carried Carrots indoors for his dinner, just as if they'd never seen him before. Carrots seemed very frightened, just as if he'd never seen them before, either!"

"That's strange!" Pepper heard Mrs Russett exclaim. "I suppose it *is* Carrots you brought in?"

"Well," laughed the farmer, "if it isn't, it must be his twin!"

"I think I'll go and see for myself," said his wife, getting up from the table.

Opening the door very carefully, so that the dogs could not get through, she went into the kitchen. There she

DADS

them on the line to dry. Then she made all the beds and put away the warm, cosy blankets till next winter.

Sleepy, who was a very adventurous little dormouse, and always had lots of good ideas, watched the washing blowing merrily on the line in the wind, and decided that it was just the day for flying a kite.

One of the baby dormice, who had a new butterfly net, wanted to go and catch butterflies, but Sleepy suddenly jumped up, and said: "We can catch butterflies tomorrow. It is such a lovely day, and the wind is just right for flying a kite. Come on."

"But, Sleepy," said one of his brothers, "we haven't got a kite."

"Oh dear," said Sleepy, looking very unhappy, and he sat down again.

"I want to catch butterflies with my new net," said the smallest dormouse again, but Sleepy had not given up the idea of the kite yet. He looked all round.

"I know," he said, "we will make one."

So while the smallest dormouse sat holding his butterfly net, the other little dormice scampered round and had soon collected all they needed—a very large leaf, a long piece of string, a short piece of string, and a lot of empty acorn shells. They threaded the acorn shells on to the short piece of string for the tail of the kite and attached the long piece of string to the leaf for them to hold.

Then they all scampered off to a place in the forest where Mr Mole had made a large mound of earth, which seemed like a mountain to the little dormice, and they all stood on the top of it, holding the kite and the butterfly net. The wind blew and blew, and nearly blew the little dormice off the top of the molehill.

Then Sleepy took hold of the end of the piece of string and, with the little ones jumping up and down with excitement, he let the kite go. Up and up went the kite, till it was far above them and there was no more string for them to unwind. The wind made the kite dance merrily on the end of the string, and all the empty acorn shells rattled together.

Then suddenly there was a very strong gust of wind. Up, up went the kite, and up and up went poor little Sleepy, still holding tightly on to the kite string.

"Help! Help!" he cried. But although all the baby dormice jumped up and down and tried to catch hold of Sleepy's feet, they could not reach, and soon Sleepy was high up in the air among the tree tops.

The little dormice just stared in amazement with open mouths. Then, altogether, they ran off down the side of the molehill, and home to tell their parents.

Mother Dormouse was horrified when she heard their tale.

"Sleepy? High up in the air on the end of the kite string?" she said. "Oh dear, whatever are we to do?"

"First things first," said Father Dormouse, putting down the paper he was reading. "Come along, and show me where you were flying the kite."

So they all trooped off through the forest to the molehill. But when they got there, there was no sign of Sleepy, or the kite. They all looked anxiously about, but he was nowhere to be seen.

Meanwhile, Sleepy had drifted further on, still holding on to the kite string. He looked down. What a lot he could see from up here. He forgot to be frightened any more. Down below he could see the old oak tree where his home was, and there were all the baby dormice running towards it. They were off to tell his Mother what had happened, he felt sure.

Further on he went, floating among the trees. 'This is great fun,' thought Sleepy to himself, never giving a thought to how he was to get down. He wished his brothers and sisters could be up here with him.

He floated on past a tree with a green door in it, and on the door it said, in large letters:

MR OWL'S HOUSE

DO NOT DISTURB

Sleepy had no intention of disturbing Mr Owl, for he knew very well that he would make a very tasty meal for a hungry owl. Hardly daring to breathe Sleepy silently

MR. OWLS HOUS
DO NOT
DISTURB
PULL

floated past the green door with the large letters. But all was well, for Mr Owl was always fast asleep during the day, after his nightly flights through the forest.

A little further on he passed by the branch of a tree, where Mrs Squirrel sat busily munching a large hazel nut.

"Hullo, Sleepy," she called. "Whatever are you doing?"

"Oh, just hanging about," said Sleepy, then laughed so much that he nearly let go of the kite string.

But Mrs Squirrel did not laugh. She could see just how much danger little Sleepy Dormouse was in as he drifted along on the kite string. Just supposing the string broke, or Sleepy let go. Oh, how dreadful! She really must go and tell Sleepy's Mother where he was, and with a whisk of her beautiful, long, bushy tail she ran off down the tree.

Still Sleepy floated on, but by now his little arms were beginning to ache, and the awful thought had struck him that he really did not know how he was going to get down. If only he could guide the kite gently to a tree,

perhaps he would be able to climb down the tree to safety. But how to reach a tree?

He tried kicking his legs, first to one side, and then the other, to see if that would steer the kite to right or left, but it only made the kite dance up and down even more in the wind, till poor Sleepy felt quite sick.

He did think he might try using one of his hands to steer with, but the thought of holding on to the kite string with only one hand was far too frightening for Sleepy. He shuddered, and decided he would have to wait and hope that help would come soon. If *only* his arms did not ache quite so much.

Then suddenly the kite stopped and, looking up, Sleepy could see that the strings of the kite were tangled in the branches of a large tree. He looked all round him. The ground seemed a very long way off. It made him feel quite funny to look down. He quickly looked up again. He tried to reach a branch of the tree, but he was hanging in mid-air and could reach neither the branch next to him, nor the branch above him.